THIS IS HOW HE LEARNED TO LOVE

Randall Brown

SONDER
PRESS

Sonder Press
New York
www.thesonderpress.com

ISBN 978-0-9997501-7-9

Cover Design: Chad Miller

First U.S. edition 2019
Printed in the USA
Distribution via Ingram

Acknowledgments

We would like to thank the following journals and magazines where some of these pieces first appeared:

Coal City Review ("Our Last Fishing Trip")
Flash: International ("Like So Many Things in That Childhood")
Pear Noir! ("Deliberately")
Necessary Fiction ("Watch")
Counterexample Poetics ("This Is How He Learned To Love")
REAL: Regarding Arts & Letters ("Skip a Life Completely")
Plain Spoke ("Equinox")
Mad Hatter's Review ("And So It Will Just Be the Two of Us")
Sou'wester ("Martian")
Redivider ("He Kept His Promises")
FRiGG ("Bounce, Wheels, Battery, Silver, Cart")
Counterexample Poetics ("The Wall The Only Thing Concrete")
Southern Indiana Review ("Graduated")
Spork Press ("Well")
Main Street Rag ("Kennings")
Straylight ("His Ghost Writer")
FRiGG ("Jupiter")
Quick Fiction ("It Doesn't")
Big Muddy ("A Sight Adjective Used to Describe a Sound")
Compass Rose ("What To Do")
FRiGG ("Myrtle")
FRiGG ("Reuben & Rosemary")
Heavy Feather Review ("She's A Stork")
Roanoke Review ("So She Just Left")
Sou'wester ("Spirits")
The Pedestal Magazine ("Plumbing")

Five Points ("Landslide")
Paddock Review ("Debt")
FRiGG ("Moments Later")
Eclectica ("Anything at All")
Adroit Journal ("Caught")
Short, Fast, and Deadly ("Boxing Day")
NANO Fiction ("To the End of Things")
Necessary Fiction ("Things")
Thumbnail ("Yes, I Knew")

for Meg, always and forever

THIS IS HOW HE LEARNED TO LOVE

Contents

Our Last Fishing Trip

THEN, IN FLAGSTAFF, A blizzard, a burp, and he talked of burgers, every few minutes another—beef, turkey, chicken, vegetable. I added bison and ostrich. We arrived an hour early, before the fishing guide, so we stared at the red canyon walls, at the condors. I mentioned the Sleestak from the old cartoon *Land of the Lost*. We shivered a bit, had expected warmth. My father wondered aloud about water and time, the river through canyon, boulders turned to sand. We pulled on waders, dressed in fishing costumes, assembled our rods. An orange scud our fly of choice according to the guidebooks. It grew later, the guide still not there, the cell phone unable to reach anyone. My father wanted to wait before moving. I waded out a bit on my own. Snow began where it should've been rain. My father whispered something I couldn't make out.

Finally, the guide, a boat hitched to his truck. "It's about time," I heard my father say. Somewhere, in between casts, on the way to a secret hole only the guide knew, or maybe on the way back to this spot, I'd say something. I'd felt it this time, the way one feels the tiniest twitch of trout, unlike rock or bottom, something entirely else.

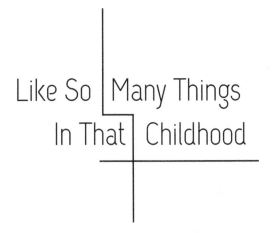

Like So | Many Things
In That | Childhood

MY FATHER PUSHED AGAINST the pedal and the dog flew up past my window as if caught in a cyclone, up and away. In the passenger seat, on that dirt road in Potter County, I swerved as the moonlight knifed into the mutt's eye—and later, when I was old and he was dying, I asked him about that dog and that drive into it, and he shook his head and said that dog, launched like rockets, still blew-up in his sleep and he was sorry, infinitely sorry, but there was nothing anyone could do about it, not now. And he looked at me for the last time and said something about anger, about it being there as long as he could remember, something inherited from his father, and I swerved from his final reach for me, told him I didn't have it, had only the knife.

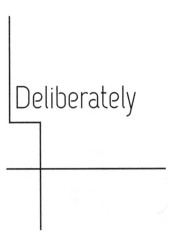

Deliberately

HE FOUND THE CONE top beer can submerged in wet clay. He scooped out the marrow, wiped the can with his shirt. Nothing remained of the label, the rest unsturdy, eaten through, but it was genuine and that mattered. Maybe his mom, a teenager, deliberately placed it, a time capsule. He set it down against the tree, continued digging. Next to him, a pen of guinea pigs left out in the sun. From under the awning his mom called out, "It wasn't my job to watch them."

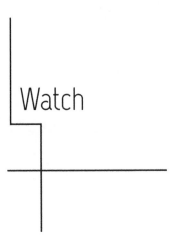

Watch

HE CLIMBS THE HILL in the snowstorm, wearing swimming goggles. At the top, he looks out at the bare birches, the grey sky, the swirl of flakes. At the bottom awaits a tree, a pond, a thicket of thorns. He holds the trashcan lid with oven mitts. A towel for a scarf. The whole way down he will look to the window for who's watching—mother, father, no one.

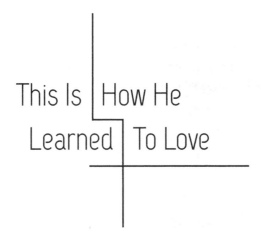

This Is | How He
Learned | To Love

HIS MOTHER'S DIAGNOSIS: NOT enough sodium in the blood. A fatally low level, if she hadn't made it to the ER, well, who knows.

"I drink a lot of seltzer," she tells the doctor. "She's an alcoholic," her son says.

"Well, yes." She picks at the bandage where the IV enters a vein. "There's also that." She promises never ever to drink again, and because it's the only time he's heard it, the doctor believes her.

"Good," the doctor says. "No more of that."

"What about rodeos?" the son asks. "Would that be okay?"

His mom laughs. What about Santa Claus? What about heaven? "It's good to have a target," the doctor says as he leaves.

At some point the doctor had mentioned a possible malignancy and now she cannot stop trembling. Maybe it's withdrawal symptoms. It could be her liver, beginning its revolt. It could be that she self-medicates to keep such anxiety at bay.

"It could be nothing," he tells his mother.

"It's certainly something." She raises her arm and the IV alarm goes off. "Oh God," she says. "There's no end to it."

They wait for the nurse to reset the cycle. The sodium will again begin its slow drip. She'll want him to stay until the trembling subsides, and because it won't, he'll have to decide.

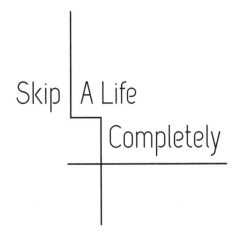

Skip A Life Completely

AFTER THE INTERVENTION, THEIR mother and her broken arm inside the detox unit, they linger in the parking lot. She asks him if he ever, you know, pills or drugs or drink. Ginger ale, he tells her, cases of it. A strange green everywhere, in the mountains and trees, like money gone through the wash. Yesterday, when they met to practice what they'd say, she'd told him it was his unlove that made their mother drink. Today, addicts walk by and who knows their sins, except there's always this, in the parking lot, the wanting to say something that sounds like sorry. He tells her that she looks too pale, asks her if she's been, you know. She sticks her finger down her throat, pretends to vomit on his shoes. Not funny, he says. No, she says, I guess not. So, she asks sometime later, do you think it's over. The thing is, he says, that choice, drink or us, she always chooses drink. Maybe it's not a choice, she says and reaches for the cigarettes, then stops. A year, two, five before they'll see each other again. She's off to the faraway coast, he downstate. Finally she says it. Sorry. It's not your fault. Any of it. He's pretending to hit baseballs over the mountains, watches them until they disappear, then turns to his sister, says, There's so little of you left.

23

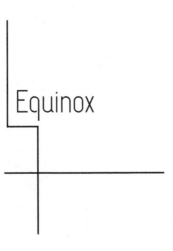

Equinox

WE PULLED THE STATION wagon into every scenic rest stop during that trip. My sister and I jostling for position on the edge between here and air. In every picture she sticks her tongue out, like that picture of Einstein plastered on college walls. Words would stick in her mind for days—and she'd shout them over the scene. She had that feathered-back haircut, parted in the middle. This is what I remember of her—leaning into space, holding her by the kneecap, the green of trees and a white steeple and the words buzzing about us.

"Archipelago!"

"Acetaminophen!"

"Fallopian Tube!"

"Geronimo!"

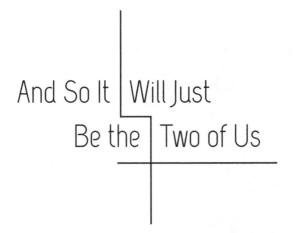

And So It | Will Just
Be the | Two of Us

MY SISTER AND I are racing the condiments. *Come on—catch-up. Wait—I must-turd. I don't relish the thought of that.* We are being given the silent treatment because yesterday we burnt down some evergreens using undergrowth and a magnifying glass. Do you understand now, my father asked before going quiet, how fire can get away? He stands at the grill, recooking the chicken; he never knows when things are done. My mother has a skin disorder that makes red welts appear wherever she puts pressure. That's how she taught me the alphabet, writing each letter with a chopstick on the underside of her forearm, waiting for letters to arise, scarlet. Tonight she shows me her arm, "Ice"—and I go inside.

In the window frame, there they all are. My sister in the burnt-out grove trying to keep the hula hoop alive, my father turning the chicken over and over, and my mother pouring from a silver flask into her Fresca.

I often think of that fire, how quickly it got out of our hands. Power. It had something to do with that: the feeling that we could affect the way things were.

It is my mom who turns to see me in the window. My sister will end up dead in high school, driving stoned. My father will join a far-off cult in the

Adirondacks, and, during an astral projection lesson, he will never return to his body.

My mother holds up her other arm. *Hurry.*

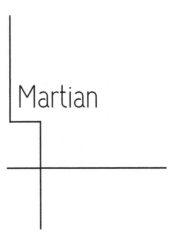

Martian

ON THE OUTSIDE OF the envelope I sent to a girl in Mars, Pennsylvania, I wrote, "Check for hidden bomb. This means you." I'd danced with her at my cousin's Bat Mitzvah but had nothing to say afterwards. I pedaled to the Hampden Township pool, sat alone on my towel reading another book about far-off worlds, while somewhere across the Susquehanna River, what I wrote, like someone yelling fire in that crowded theater, evacuated a building, sent sirens from East Shore to West Shore.

My name crackled into the space above the pool summoning me to the office. There, two guys dressed like the agents from *Close Encounters* waited with questions meant to make me crumble, and once I saw the shred of envelope, I confessed. They wanted remorse, so I gave them tears and sorrys and the shakes, but after they left, I rode home in a rush, a Willie Stargell card in the spokes like the beat of a song, and I knew what I wanted: to capture its notes, send them off, wait for the call of sirens, crying out, "Here I am. Here I am. I am here."

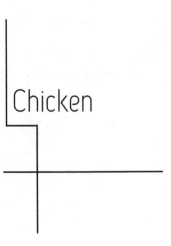

Chicken

HIS MOTHER KNEELS AMONG the clover, looking for the bottle opener. He, at the bottom of hill, under the awning, lines up beer bottles for Evil Knievel to jump over.

"Race me," he yells out.

"Leave me alone," she yells back.

He builds a trench in the grass, fills it with water, pretends the Snake River of some faraway canyon has twisted its way to him.

"Race me!"

"Jesus! Leave me alone."

In mid-air, Evil gets himself in a real pickle, running out of rocket power. He wants to eject, but he's no chicken, so down he goes into the disappearing river, into the mud.

"Race me!"

"Fuck off!"

It's late now.

"Race me!"

"Okay, okay. Jeez fucking Louise."

He meets her in the clover, says "1-2-3. Go!"

She goes. He sticks out his foot and she falls hard, all the way down the hill into the Snake River, next to Evil and his million broken bones.

He Kept
His Promises

HE DROVE NONSTOP FROM California to Philly to take me to the Zembo circus. He talked a Shriner out of his fez hat, called me the Spaceman. He brought uncirculated coins, waited for me to take out the magnifying glass he'd sent me for my birthday, explained the mint marks to me, the S for San Francisco. I sometimes used the glass to melt soldiers with the sun, lined them up on my dresser. He called them the Veterans of the Magnifying Glass Wars, made up stories for each one. For one-armed Hank, a softball pitcher with a windmill wind-up, and for No-Face Saul, with a closetful of masks. He kept a pocket of See Candies even though he was diabetic, and I ate popcorn because I was allergic to most things. Motorcycles in a steel cage roared above us, their tail pipes shooting out fire, and still I could hear my grandfather's snores. I held his hand. It felt worn, like an old catcher's mitt, his fingers trembling like the earth out West. I whispered something to him as a man shot out of a cannon and clowns tumbled in and out of too-small cars and bears danced with balls on their noses. It wasn't "wake up," but something else. I wore the magnifying glass like a monocle. Everything blurred. He woke startled, to an elephant's trumpet, and I said, Pap, did you hear that? He said he did, and it was a fine thing to say. He'd always remember it.

Bounce, Wheels, Battery, Silver, Cart

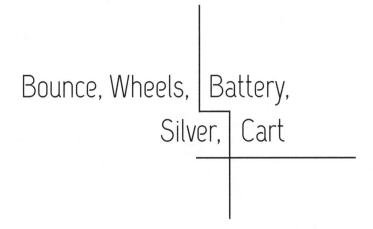

HE BOUGHT IT WITH the $100 bill his grandfather willed to him, the battery too, silver paint. He stole tires off the abandoned wheelbarrows. Down the hill, toward the water, he bounced. First at night, then always, he saw death. He neared the flooded creek, hand on the brake. In the painting over his grandfather's desk Charon wielded his oar like a club—and everyone cowered as if alive. The boy yanked on the handle and the cart spun, tossing him out. The cart floated, then sank, and he didn't cry, not even then, for the world was as it was.

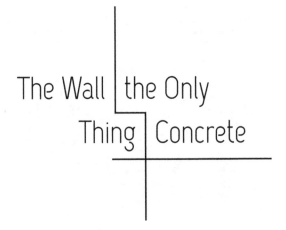

The Wall the Only Thing Concrete

THE PSYCHOLOGY TEACHER WRAPPED bandanas around our eyes, had us walk down the halls, tapping a cane. Later, we held onto our blindness, the creek so cold that even the air cracked. We stepped onto the ice. We clasped hands. We went in circles. We didn't care about what we couldn't see.

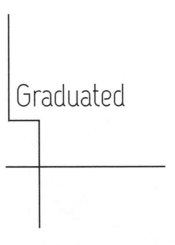

Graduated

WE BUILT A GRAVITY Bong with a 3-liter Thirstbuster, a bucket and a bowl screwed into the top. We sprinkled cocaine on the bong hits, called them Cocoa Puffs. This one time Noah stood up, and like an airplane in a roll, glided across the entire room into a plate glass window. We told the police it was a rock. They had lots of questions about this rock. How big was it? Who had thrown it? Marc hinted at ghosts. After they left, we took the Gravity Bong out of the ceiling. Noah, remarkably, did not have a single cut on him. Maybe Noah was the ghost. We smoked until we forfeited substance for the ethereal. We floated out windows. We haunted halls. We floated into the offices of buildings and stuck there, balloons to a wall.

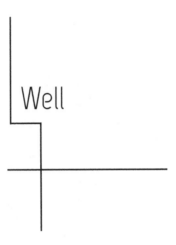

Well

FOR SIX MONTHS NOW her legs ache, a persistent fog, a fever that never rises above 100.2. My daughter calls her the ghost; my son, just "Sick." She tries to find the trail back to before, but there's no answer there. I want to tell her to believe she will come back to us, as if that's all it will take.

There's no bounce in this house. We glide on socks. My daughter whispers that we cannot wake the undead. Days before she fell ill my son was promised a trip to New York. He talks of his rotten luck. I tell him he needs E.T. to descend upon him, teach him empathy. His sister says it will take more than that. Fights that once ended with slaps and slammed doors fizzle out into whispered hisses.

Groceries, dishes, laundry, a helmet for horseback riding camp, a tennis racquet to be strung, dogs to feed and walk, rooms to unclutter.

I bring her matzo ball soup and crackers. My wife once told my daughter that the matzo roamed Israeli deserts, a giant and fierce predator. She told my son, at age three, that he ran on batteries. How they screamed.

She sips the broth. I am on the edge of the bed, watching the goslings. Some nights there's the unending shriek of the babies' cries. Foxes live in the abandoned well near the pond.

It isn't about you, I tell myself again.

41

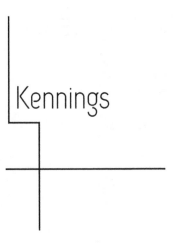

Kennings

A SWORD BECOMES A compound, wound-hoe. A ship transforms to wave-steed, the ocean to whale-road.

The clouds transform to sky-curtains, butterflies to silk-kites. The day to candle-snuffer. The dusk to shadow-meld. The kids to Andersen-Flemmings.

A marriage to dream-swallower. A house to silence-shelter. Separated. Rearranged.

Sky-Shelter. Candle-Kites. Flemming-Wound. Anderson-Snuffer. Dream-Silence.

His Ghost Writer

HE MEETS ME AT the gate. He wants to know if I am the writer. I tell him yes, that would be I. He wants to know what I expect, and I say what the ad said: good pay, a place to live. He shakes my hand. As we walk, he whittles his nails with a penknife. He's become ungainly and sad and can no longer land the roles he once had.

My son used to tell me this joke, about a mouse who snuck into a house, drank all the wine, ate all the baked beans, listened to Elvis until the people came home. They're angry, the people, about the wine, the baked beans, the messed-up Elvis records. Who did this? The mouse stumbles out of his hole, hiccups, farts, mumbles, "I'm all shook up."

I will live in his house, drink his Chianti, inhabit his life. This man who hadn't fallen asleep under the umbrella while his son circled the bottom of the spa, in that endless way that kids drown, and tell jokes, and laugh at things long after they are funny.

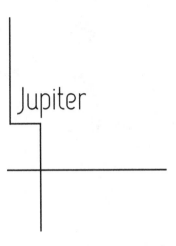

Jupiter

A PRAYING MANTIS, NOT a robin, came that Spring—an elongated alien, ready for worship. They contemplated one another that afternoon, until they were both in shadow. He knew a lot about mantises, fascinated with them since childhood. In folk tales, they directed lost children back home. He'd never seen one, except in books, until now.

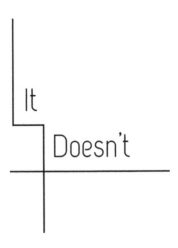

It Doesn't

THEY COME UP TO tell me what a good person I am, for letting the cook's daughter swim with us. The girls build a village of sand hamlets—a man carries chairs, sets them up, covers each one with a towel, adjusts the umbrella. I ask him about his own kids. They live in Canada with their mother while he works. It must be hard, I say and press money into his hand. He can't thank me enough. The same with the woman bringing me the mango-banana daquiri. I make a joke about wanting a tiny umbrella, and she returns with one and some pineapple and cherries. The girls build a moat to protect their town. I read the condensed *New York Times*, listen to an Elton John playlist. A chicken now and then runs from the bushes to the gravel to the sand and then back. Someone wants to know if it bothers me. He will kill the chicken if it does.

A Slight | Adjective Used
To Describe | a Sound

EACH DAY, HE HEARS less. He has new thoughts, about what blind people dream, about the city, silent and lit like a ghost. He will have to remember: his wife's whisper, his daughter's giggle, songs. Already, his wife emails him from downstairs, already he's online teaching. They can find no reason. Maybe it will stop. He goes away for some days and is lonely by the sea, wet from the spray. Frost began a poem with "the shattered waves made a misty din," a mixing of senses: the waves, not the din, should be misty.

He'd thought that his last name meant pear tree but today someone told him it meant oak, or folk. Cats roam the bushes here. He says cat tail as if it were a plant. He can't stop saying cat tail. Even his inner voice says it, and he wonders about that voice, if that's all there will be. Eventually. Event. He never noticed that before, the event in eventually. The shattered waves. Misty din. He gets stuck on such things.

Someone makes her way out of one of the cottages on the hill. She wears the white bathrobe from the resort. She smokes a cigar.

She says something. He points to his ears, shakes his head. She moves out to him on the rocks.

"It's early to be yelling," she yells.

51

She wears the bathrobe sash like a scarf, coughs and spits red onto the rocks. She says something that is either "trying" or "dying." He says something that is either sorry or worry.

They talk like this for a bit—and then she makes a motion to leave. She throws the cigar in the water. He stills himself, all focus, bent on hearing its rusty sizzle.

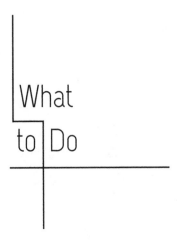

What to Do

I WONDERED IF THE old woman collected stray children as one would cats. *So many children, she didn't know what to do.* The picture of the shoe showed a playground built into its tongue and happy face after happy face slipping down the slide, peeking out the windows, leaning against the heel. In one window, bread seemed to be cooling. But there was no bread, only broth. How plump and round the artist drew them! Each of those so many children she whipped soundly. I didn't understand soundly but imagined it be like a stick against skin, or a stick against air on the back swing. This verse haunted me at night, my mother out and my father crying like a kitten in the room next to mine. My mother had only one kid and didn't know what to do. Her shoes made the tiniest tap up the stairs after my father had fallen off to sleep. She never once looked in on me to see if I were there, even if I coughed or sniffed real loud. She slept soundly, until noon, while I counted the children, the bowls of broth, each thwack of the old woman's switch until it felt as if I were among them. And at the end, when she put them to bed, I could imagine them happy, I really could.

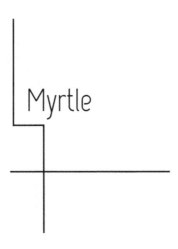

Myrtle

THE OPTOMETRIST MENTIONED HIS divorce during her screening. Out of his office, she fiddled with frames. They ended up, that first Friday, at a gallery in Old City. She couldn't see what he saw in the canvas. Every time she picked up another glass of wine, he said, "If you give a mouse a cookie...."

At Blue, he had his drink. A cocktail, Grey Goose with juice and maybe Triple Sec. He had big eyes. She took to calling him Dr. Eckleberg, and he never asked why. She wanted to explain that it came from *Gatsby*, that his billboard looked over an ash heap, that the Dutch sailors came upon the green breast of a new world, full of white wonder, and now look! Look at what's become of things!

And this became *their* thing, these first Fridays, the galleries and cocktails and abstract paintings, the give a mouse a cookie line and the "Good night, Dr.Eckleberg," and her hoping, just once, he'd wonder why.

Reuben & Rosemary

HE INTRODUCED HER TO slant rhymes, for *orange* and *porridge*, and she wondered at first if it were enough that her menus nearly rhymed, if *waffle* and *falafel* truly inclined to each other naturally or if it were forced upon them, until one day it didn't matter, when *beans* and *steamed* met, slanted, like *ham steak* and *pancake*, *radish* and *sandwich*, the waitress who loved rhyme with her toast and the man at the counter who loved her almost.

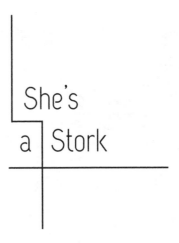

She's
a Stork

AND THAT MAKES IT ungraceful to bowl. The only thing falling for her here are pins, and not that many. She drinks seven Shirley Temples! That's a lot of cherries. "Look at this one," she says. "I don't think it's supposed to be purple." Later, she mentions that kegler sounds like exercises to tighten, well you know, muscles, for women? She doesn't make a dent, so she goes outside. She thinks "Everyone is damaged" and knows it's not a new thought in the world, but, as the thrift store across the street advertises, "It's new to her." How might this idea change everything? In her car, she lights the bowl, and comes to some understanding that won't last. It has something to do with bowling, that's for certain, and that in another place, a different atmosphere, she might be a star.

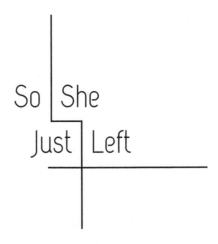

So She Just Left

SHE FOUND A TOOTH in her burger, said nothing. She thought of making a joke, something about smiling, saying cheese. She didn't. She sat against the booth, heard her brother's voice, be sure not to slouch. The man kept talking about leveraged bonds. Suddenly silence—and she almost jumped. He had asked her something of herself. She made up a story about the tooth, how she carried it with her, a baby tooth, hers, one the tooth fairy left or forgot about. He asked to see it, but she knew she'd be revealed then. He'd examine it, say, "Rat."

Spirits

"THIS," MARY YELLED TO him, "is what I call an untamed jukebox." The Cure as AI with Carl Perkins on the backside.

At the Outer Inn, the Iron Lobster, Ma's Fine Dining, he'd spent his childhood, with his mom's own bar-wide announcements, like those of Miss Mary Blue, a White Russian dangling from her lips. "Nostalgia," the bar sign announced, "isn't what it used to be."

Mary made her way over to him. Mary Christmas. Mary Queen of Scots. Mary Me. His mother always chose Nat "King" Cole, that merry old soul, and he'd watch her dance with the guys he'd become. Is this what drew him back—the wish of an eight-year-old on a bar stool to matter more than Maker's Mark and a stranger who smelled like smoke and Old Spice?

Mary Blue took hold of him, pushed them together, happy new year! "Resolution, resolution!" An incantation.

He shouted back, "Decompose! Disintegrate! Disperse!" Mary Blue took a flight out, fluttering hummingbird-like at the window, the bar faded back into the wood panels of the basement, someone dropped the ball in New York City, and he blew on his noisemakers, one after another.

Plumbing

SHE WANTS TO SEE the bucket of sludge from the upstairs sink. Dazzling, she says. She offers him coffee from a machine, explains each sound: the grinding of the beans, the tamping of the grounds, the pre-brewing, brewing, bubbling of steam to make foam. He holds the wire snake, unsure of its place, of lines to be crossed. She says there's a lilt about him, and the only thing that comes to mind is a song from a black and white movie, "Good Time Coming." She says her husband hates the machine, its noise and bulkiness; she has the coffee waiting for him after he showers. The plumber takes his own taste, understands now the origin of the black sludge in the bathroom sink. Wonders if it is love that makes him pour each cup into the drain. Or something altogether else.

Landslide

SOMEWHERE FARAWAY A LANDSLIDE buries parents and their kids. In the next days they will attach sound equipment to the gaps and listen. Eventually, they will make the assessment to call off the search. I know I should be sad. I know all about mourning. I am like the majority, going about the day, struggling with silly things, like the line at the post office, wondering how long I can stand it, that feeling of being trapped, willing myself to stay.

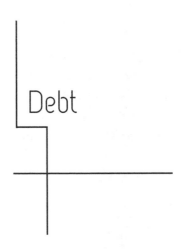

Debt

I SIT THE KIDS in the family room, start talking about the 1979 Pirates, how they'd won a championship with this song "We are Family" by Sister Sledge. I tell Rachel I don't know what a sledge is; I tell Noah I'm getting to the point.

I say I'm trying to tell them how their grandmother wanted a *Cosmopolitan* magazine; the final game of the series was on; there weren't DVDs or other ways to see it again. She told me I had to bike to the Pensupreme to get this magazine. She wouldn't let up, ended up trying to drag me up the stairs by my hair.

You want us to hate her, Noah says. Rachel wants to know if I got her the magazine.

Yes, I tell her. But it was the wrong month, one she already had.

And? Noah asks.

I went back, got her the right one.

I would never do that, he says. That's because you're mean, Rachel tells him.

I paid for it with paper route money, I tell them. And that's why I can't just give you the money for iTunes.

Whatever, Noah says. He'll clean his room, though, if it matters that much. And Rachel will fold laundry, maybe take the dinner dishes away.

They're both sorry they asked.

Stargell would stand at the plate, swing that bat like a windmill. I didn't have to get that magazine, but I did.

I wanted the world to owe me something.

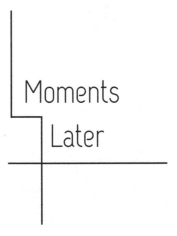

Moments Later

HE SHOVED THE BRANCH between the gates of Eden, leaning on it with all his new-found weight, as if the gates could be unframed. He pushed harder until the stick snapped like bone.

"Serpents!" he cried out. "It's lost," she said.

He had written a poem. Maybe orange and oriole had rhyming mates then. A poem written in a world full of unborn desire. It must've been a very Eastern poem, describing the world as it is rather than what it might mean. He'd written it upon a leaf that held fast to the tree and could not fall.

"Forget it," he said. He tossed the stick to the ground.

"It held something," she said.

"I said forget it. Let's go." He pulled at her, bone of his bone, flesh of his flesh.

She stood fast in her new clothes, her skirt like a balloon. In the distance, a meteor scorched the sky, left silence—man and woman—a world they had no names for.

Anything at All

KIPPER, OUR KING CHARLES Cavalier, wakes me up with "Cheerio!" In the afternoon, he asks for tea and crumpets, calls me "Guv'nor." It's been this way for the past three days, since the wife and kids left for Santa Domingo without me. It'll take a while for me to adjust to the new medicine, my last chance before some kind of institution, no shit. It's come to this. Somewhere my wife backstrokes with her parents in an infinity pool, the chef serves them a holiday shepherd's pie, the kids float in the ocean, wave to cruise ships. I'm a million miles from them, in winter, out by the covered pool and dead trees, the King Charles chasing doves while someone sings "Feed the Birds." I'm scared, terrified. "Wish me luck," I say to Kipper. "Bugger off," he barks. I have to keep the anxiety at bay, accept uncertainty, stop fleeing and hiding away from a world I can't control. I see worms, or is it grass, or is it an old acid trip, aneurysm, stroke or nothing, nothing, fuck. Don't try to make it stop; don't push the panic away. Accept it. Let it in. Okay. All the birds chased away, Kipper leaps on my chest, stares at me. He has such a small head. All fluff, like Winnie the Pooh. He curls up and falls asleep in the crook of my neck. I want a head like that, I say to him. I'd give anything for it.

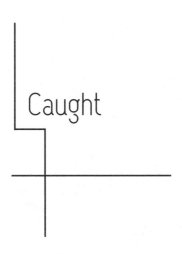

Caught

THAT THANKSGIVING, MY UNCLE Nate's esophagus could only handle sour cream. Even then, he threw it up, off the back porch. Afterward, he saw me, throwing a ball against a garage door, inning after imagined inning. He could barely talk, so he had to walk over, lean into my ear. He told me that's the way to be, never dependent on anyone. He said when the silver angels came down with their subpoena, he wondered how he'd be judged, his own punishment a derivative of some yet unknown variable. And this worried him immensely because he'd killed Germans, lots of them. He told me to wait, left, came back with a baseball glove. You, my son, are a catalyst for change, he told me, then whipped the ball hard. It exploded into my hand. I didn't flinch. I returned it to him hard, hard enough to bring tears and bile, harder than he'd ever figured.

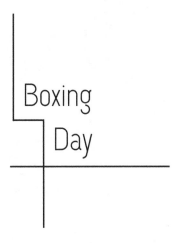

Boxing Day

THE ISLAND NIGHT BROUGHT out so many stars that it looked more like snowmelt than sky. One could point anywhere into the air and make a constellation, call it whatever came to mind. Look: "lost mitten." Back at the villa, he wrapped boxes for the staff, but they ended up offended. He wasn't sure if it had to do with the present inside—umbrellas that fit inside pockets—or the idea of the present itself. Wherever he went, he ended up floundering. Along the beach, a security guard stopped him, told him he had strayed beyond the bounds of the villa owners' property. Stars, the Hollywood kind, flickered on that beach. He lay on his back at the boundary. A long time ago, it didn't matter that the starry sky held only questions; now the security guard stood over him. He asked what he'd done wrong, and the guard pointed away from that beach, asked him if he needed help finding his way home. Beyond the guard, he glimpsed the stars, fallen to that beach, those long-ago wishes clinging, still.

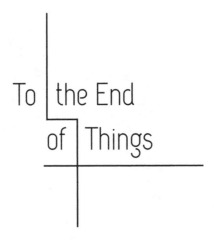

To the End of Things

WE MET ON A Sunday for sundaes. Right out she said she belonged to a group. I think she wanted to jar me. The group, she said, believed the world was flat. It could be worse—signals from space she received on her radio, or maybe through her spine into her skull. That's usually a deal-breaker, she said. I winked, not sure what a wink would mean. She seemed to like it. We walked down Armitage, and I wondered if this was what it meant to be un-lonely. I don't know, she answered. I hadn't known I'd said it aloud. She bumped against me a lot. Helicopter-leaves whirled around us and I thought of gravity: how feathers and rocks fall at the same rate but only in vacuums, in worlds unlike our own. We looked in windows. The painting of a grotesque woman gnarled like tree knots spooked me and sent me running down an alley. I thought I'd once again ruined something, but she'd run, too. Now we have something we can laugh about, she said. I asked her where we were going, walking like this, and she took hold of me and pulled me along.

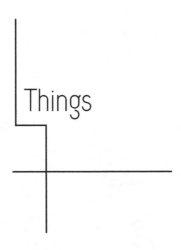

Things

THE CAVEMAN FILLED THE cave to overflowing: tiger ribs, petrified branches, reflective rocks, feathers of burnt purples and reds. He referred to the cave as stocked; his wife had other names she kept to herself. Maybe he didn't want a wife, but an assistant, to sort what he'd hunted and gathered. She wanted to know where they'd sleep, and he shrugged, pointed anywhere to that mountainside, cave after cave after empty cave.

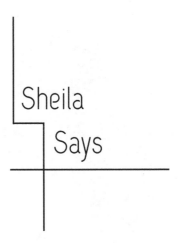

Sheila Says

SHEILA WRITES EVERYTHING ON her arms. *Six o'clock dinner with Carol. Must pay Cheryl. New Depp film. Remember, world was flat once.* While she sleeps, I write *Marry Alex*, but in the morning, she scrubs it away along with *Plath's a fraud* & *Tennis at 2:30.* For her birthday, I'll buy her a box of permanent markers. She'll buy Brillo pads.

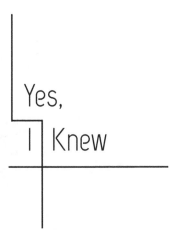

Yes,
I Knew

I RAN INTO HER, wrapped against the winter like a Russian peasant, in Germantown, her dog pulling her across the street almost into a bus to see me. The first thing she said: "Are you still so blue?" I had crouched to greet the happy spaniel, wriggling to get in my arms. "I guess I am," I answered. The spaniel's eyes leaked continually, a strange stink I'd missed without realizing. In a portrait of the young, lonely Queen Victoria, she holds her spaniel Dash as if he is the only thing she loves in this world. She even left her coronation early to run home to bathe him. "Where you headed?" I asked, and she pointed East; I pointed West, to the river path, now on my back, the spaniel on my chest, licking everywhere, his tongue and breath creating a fog. "Oh, that's so sad," she said. "I mean—I had no idea. How much he missed you. Oh, just look at him. Did you even know?" When I'd be up at night he'd find me, and we'd throw a ball into the kitchen for hours. I would tell him things, things I couldn't tell her, and then we'd go out by the pool, walk in circles. I would shake my head, over and over, trying to get all those thoughts out, those dark, black ones. But I couldn't shake it, whatever it was. And he'd just wag his tail, stick by my side, walking, fetching, tilting his tiny head, trying so hard to get it.

Author Note

Randall Brown is the author of the award-winning collection *Mad to Live*, his essay on (very) short fiction appears in *The Rose Metal Field Guide to Writing Flash Fiction:Tips from Editors, Teachers, and Writers in the Field*, and he appears in *Best Small Fictions* 2015, 2017, & 2019 and The Norton Anthologies *New Micro: Exceptionally Short Fiction* & *Hint Fiction*. He founded and directs FlashFiction.Net and has been published and anthologized widely, both online and in print. Recent book include the prose poetry collection *I Might Never Learn* (Finishing Line Press 2018) and the novella *How Long is Forever* (Running Wild Press 2018). He is also the founder and managing editor of Matter Press and its *Journal of Compressed Creative Arts*. He received his MFA in Fiction from Vermont College.

CPSIA information can be obtained
at www.ICGtesting.com
Printed in the USA
BVHW071104260120
570530BV00001B/159